THE NILE FILES

Stories about Ancient Egypt

THE SCRUNCHY SCARAB

by Philip Wooderson

Illustrations by Andy Hammond

FRANKLIN WATTS

NEW YORK • LONDON • SYDNEY

First published in 2000 by Franklin Watts
96 Leonard Street, London EC2A 4XD

Text © Philip Wooderson 2000
Illustrations © Andy Hammond 2000

The right of Philip Wooderson to be identified as
the Author of this Work has been asserted by
him in accordance with the Copyright, Designs
and Patents Act, 1988

Editor: Lesley Bilton
Designer: Jason Anscomb
Consultant: Dr Anne Millard, BA Hons, Dip Ed, PhD

A CIP catalogue record for this book
is available from the British Library

ISBN 0 7496 3649 1 (hbk)
0 7496 3653 X(pbk)

Dewey Classification 932

Printed in Great Britain

(ONTENTS

QUIZ (to be completed before reading this book)

Life in Ancient Egypt depended on one crucial thing. What was it?

a)   Building more pyramids
b)   Pharaoh not losing his temper
c)   The River Nile

CLUE Egypt was nothing but desert – except for a narrow strip kept fertile by the River Nile flooding its banks once a year. Everyone lived next to the Nile, all food was grown near the Nile, and everything that was traded went up and down the Nile.

ANSWER

It's 'b'

← Pharaoh

Got it right? Jump on board for the journey and learn some more funny facts about Ancient Egypt.

Dawn on the River Nile in the reign of the Great Armenlegup – known as the Fearful Pharaoh.

Ptoni woke with a start. Something itchy and creepy was trying to crawl up his nose.

He'd slept on deck, as usual, wrapped up in a piece of old linen. His Dad's boat, *Hefijuti*, had been moored overnight in the rushes. Dad was still fast asleep, but the rest of the crew were wide awake, slurping up their breakfast.

Ptoni sniffed. What *was* it? Something itchy and twitchy that made him sniffle and snort and –

"CHOO!"

A nasty black thing shot into the air. It

* Yes, beer was drunk through a straw – see page 60

bounced off the mast, hit the deck and whirred about upside down with its little legs wriggling away. It was a big black bug! Ptoni jumped up with a yell, ready to stamp on the thing. He already had a pet snake, a scorpion in an old beer pot, and a couple of scrawny rats he'd saved from the ship's cat, Ptiddles.

Dad opened one eye. "Wow, Ptoni – that's a scarab beetle! If you look after him he'll bring us lots of luck, and things will go well for the voyage!"

Hmmm. They could do with some luck, but Ptoni wasn't sure that a beetle was going to bring it.

They'd just sailed up from the coast, where Dad had been so amazed to see all that open sea that he'd bought a whole cargo of planks without noticing that they were riddled with woodworm.

The crew, with much grumbling, had chopped it up for Dad to trade as firewood. And all he'd got in return were a few dozen baskets of figs, as dry as withered eyeballs, and thirty jumbo-sized flasks of out-of-date, greasy palm oil.

Yes. They could do with some luck.

"Right, lads," Dad called out. "When you're ready?"

The lads were taking their time. They hadn't been paid for weeks. They yawned. They leaned on their oars. But finally they got *Hefijuti* drifting out midstream, just as a convoy of galleys came surging round the bend.

"Wow–eee!!!" Dad was so impressed he let go of the steering oar.

Horns blared and voices shouted. "Make way for the obelisk barge. We bring stone for Pharaoh's temple!"

"Not another temple," shouted one of the lads. "How many temples has he got now?"

"Too many."

BEEEEEEEEEEP!

Ptoni grabbed Dad's oar. *Hefijuti* lurched to the left, missing the leading galley by the length of one of Ptiddle's whiskers. Then the boat got caught in the wash. Bump! *Hefijuti* stopped dead.

"Wow, *now* what's happened?" asked Dad.

"I think we're stuck in the mud."

"Get out and push, lads!" Dad ordered.

"You first," said one of the lads.

Ptoni pointed at the crocodiles swimming in the water. "I think we're going to need help, Dad."

At last another boat came gliding round the bend. This was a large sleek galley with billowing sails, and a canopy over the rear deck to shade a fat man on a throne. He was lounging back on cushions, popping grapes into his mouth and spitting the pips over the side.

"Is that the Pharaoh?" gasped Ptoni.

"No, stupid," jeered one of the lads. "Look

at the size of him. It's a fat tax collector.*
Ahoy there, Your Scribeship! Could you give
us a tow?"

The galley swept on downstream without a
single person on board even giving them a
sideways glance.

"Oh dear," said Dad. "Now what?"

"We wait," said Ptoni.

They waited. The sun got hotter and
hotter, and was high in the sky before another
boat came bobbing round the bend.

---

* Tax collectors had very good jobs – see page 61

It was small, overloaded, and stank of over-ripe melons, but everyone waved and shouted, and the man on board waved back.

"Can't stop," he called. "I'm late for the market at Feruka."

"Could you give us a lift?" yelled Dad.

"Not with this cargo – we'd sink." The man looked more closely at Dad. "I might do a deal, though. What are you offering?"

"Thirty baskets of figs," said Dad.

"But that's all the figs we've got, Dad," Ptoni said. "They're worth more than *all* his melons!"

"Done," said the man. "Thirty baskets of

figs and I'll give you a ride for FREE. Can't say fairer than that, chief!"

In no time *Hefijuti* was heaped up with squashy melons. Ptoni and Dad scrambled onto the other boat and perched on the baskets of figs. They waved goodbye to the lads, who seemed strangely distressed.

"What's that the boy's holding?" asked the boatman.

Dad winked. "Our lucky scarab."

"Yeah? It's been lucky for me, too. Today's the feast of Thoth, so figs ought to go down a treat."

"Why's that?"

"You don't know much," said the boatman. "Haven't you seen the statue of the god Thoth at the temple? He looks like a baboon.* And all baboons like figs, right? So folks will want to take figs as an offering to the temple. Much better than stinky old melons!"

Dad looked glum.

"Cheer up," said the boatman. "Just pop the bug in this box. I'll give him some figs to munch, and let's hope that he brings more luck."

Around the next bend, there was the town. They could see lots of small

* Egyptians were fond of baboons – see page 62

mud houses, some warehouses and a temple.
There was also a single great gleaming palace.
It had a huge walled garden and its own
landing stage, with a swish boat tied alongside,
as big as the tax collector's galley.

"Wow! Who owns all *that*?" asked Dad.

"That's Kashpot's place," said the
boatman, lowering his voice.

"Who's Kashpot?"

"The swankiest, richest, craftiest merchant
in Feruka. If you want to get lucky, mate, don't
get mixed up with that rogue."

They moored the boat at the town quay.

The market was in full swing, bustling with noisy people stocking up for the feast of Thoth. Dad settled down to watch while Ptoni helped the boatman to unload the figs. Business was soon brisk.

"Those sales could have been ours," said Ptoni.

Dad sighed. "Never mind. Let's sit down and wait for a sign from the Gods telling us what we ought to do next."

"Find someone with a big boat, Dad, to pull us off the mudbank."

"Oh yeah? That's the easy bit, Ptoni. How

will we pay them? With melons?"

"We've still got the palm oil, Dad. Come on. Let's ask around."

They asked at three different stalls. "Do you know anyone with a big boat who'd be interested in thirty flasks of the very best palm oil?"

"I guess we should take their advice, and go with the flow," said Dad.

They went with the flow of the crowd through the market towards Kashpot's palace. But Dad found so much to look at that he was soon lagging behind. There were stalls heaped with all sorts of foods, farm tools, rolls of fabric, pans, jewellery and beads. Ptoni doubled back and caught Dad staring into a seedy workshop with a painted sign outside –

WIDOW WIGNITE'S COOLING CONES

– hot from Memphis. Put one on top of your wig. Your friends will go crazy with envy!

Dad wanted to try on a cone. Then he wanted to buy one.

"What for?" asked Ptoni crossly. "You don't even wear a wig."

WIDOW WIGNITE'S COOLING CONES

The helpful assistant moved closer. "For everybody who's *any*-body, they're simply MUST HAVES for smart parties," she said, grabbing Dad's last bangle for payment.

"I'll give it to Kashpot. He'll *love* it," said Dad.

Ptoni wasn't so sure, but before he could voice any doubts the warehouse door crashed open. Out came the fat tax collector, aloft on a mobile throne carried by four helpers. A weaselly assistant trotted after them, almost hidden by a pile of rolled-up scrolls, and he was followed by eight more guards carrying crates on their heads.

"Get back, you lousy rabble!" A guard shoved Ptoni so hard he was knocked to the ground. His scarab box got kicked from his hand and went skidding into a ditch.

Ptoni gulped. What a stink – the ditch was an open sewer! But he needed to get his scarab back, so that it could bring them good luck. Taking a deep breath he lowered himself over the edge.

The water came up to his ankles. This wouldn't have been too bad, except that the water was muddy, and the mud wasn't nice clean mud.

As he reached for his box in the slime, he heard the tax collector shouting. "Help me down off my throne, Ferrut. I'm too full of Widow Wignite's beer. It's thirsty work collecting taxes, but luckily here's a ditch."

Ptoni crouched in the mud with his scarab
box, not feeling in the least bit lucky.

"You let Widow Wignite off too lightly,
sire," Ferrut said peevishly.

"I'm saving her up for next year." The tax
collector burped. "Besides she gave me a few
hints, over a goblet or three, concerning
Kashpot. I think we'll go to him now and sting
him for all he's got. Then I'll take the rest of

the day off to enjoy the feast." He hiccuped.
"Don't just stand there. Help me back onto my
throne, toe-rag."

Ptoni counted up to ten and then scrambled
out of the ditch. Dad would have to be nifty
and do his deal with Kashpot before the tax
collector turned up. But where was Dad now?
Ptoni hurried along looking in all directions,
until he reached the entry to Kashpot's palace.
Would Dad have gone in by himself?

The wall was too high to peer over, so Ptoni asked a servant who was guarding the entrance if his Dad had gone into the palace.

"A dreamy sort of chap, carrying a funny hat?" asked the guard.

"That sounds like him."

The guard called to another servant, but she wouldn't let Ptoni indoors until he had washed all the smelly gunge off his arms and legs. Then she led him upstairs to a large room with pillars and painted walls. Dad was chatting away with a smooth-looking man in swish sandals.

DESIGNER LOGO

TRENDY TRAINING SANDALS

Ptoni wasted no time. "Kashpot, sire," he blurted, "the tax collector's coming, and he's going to sting you."

"No way," said the smooth man, beaming at Ptoni. "You see, my name's Phixit. I see to all Master's wishes and Mistress Nofret's whims. Master is busy adjusting his scrolls now."

"But," Ptoni turned to Dad, who was still holding his cone, "you need to get Kashpot's help quickly before he –"

"Relax," said Dad, smiling lazily. "I've already talked to Kashpot. He told me to keep my cone, but he's offered to help with our boat, and take all our oil – in return for a few bales of linen."

Ptoni swallowed. "Only a *few*?"

"Eight or nine?"

"Dad, that's robbery."

"Stop talking business, Ptoni. We're looking at Works of Art."

"We've just had these done," said Phixit, waving at the murals painted on the wall. "This one shows Master's new country villa. Such a beautiful garden. Don't you love the pomegranate trees? And, as you can see from this next scene," Phixit moved down the room,

"he likes to have lots of guests to share *the* most fabulous feasts."

The Master starred large in each picture. He was wearing the chunkiest jewels and the most crazy cool cones, but Ptoni couldn't stop himself. "He's just like a fat baboon!"

There was a sharp intake of breath from Phixit. "Funny you should say that. Master

himself had noticed that he looks rather like the statue of the god Thoth at the temple. So, as he wasn't at home when the artist came, I took the painter to see it and told him not to be shy of making Master look properly – *godly*."

KNOCK! KNOCK!

"We all know who *that* is!" said Phixit, trotting across the room to pick up a large pair of cymbals.

Clash–CLASH–CLASH–Clash.

At once hordes of servants rushed in and

OPERATION TAX COLLECTOR!

dashed about the room grabbing pots, vases and cushions, which they stuffed into wooden chests. Then they covered the chests with rough sacks, while Phixit drew some drab hangings over the bright new murals.

A door at the far end opened and a pretty young woman came out, holding a screaming baby in a linen sling.

"I've taken my jewels off, Phixit, but where shall I hide them?"

"Don't fret, Mistress Nofret. I'll hide them in the very last place the tax collector will think of looking."

He was stuffing her bangles and bracelets into the baby's sling when Kashpot huffed down the stairs. He was just like the baboon in the murals, except he looked twenty years older.

"Phixit, what are you up to? We can't have Heebi Jeebi making that sort of racket in front of that toad of a tax collector!"

Heebi Jeebi screamed louder than ever, but

Kashpot started to smile. He stepped forward holding out both his hands.

"Ah, Your Eminence Grubbiflub. Welcome back to my humble home."

CHAPTER 5
DAD DOES HIS STUFF

The tax collector shuffled forward, backed by Ferrut and his bodyguards. They were all grinning like hungry hyenas.

"What's humble about this palace? It looks even swankier than it did last year." He burped. "You must be raking it in."

"How you love to tease," laughed Kashpot. "We've had a dreadful year. Nothing but droughts and locusts. We're down to our last

few beans. Though, as you are such an old friend, we hope you'll do us the honour of sharing our measly meal."

Grubbiflub's fleshy nostrils twitched as he breathed in the smell of roast meats from the kitchens. "Tax collecting in this heat is hungry and *thirsty* work."

Nofret gave him a brilliant smile. "Perhaps sire would care for a quenching drink before he gets down to work?"

Grubbiflub leered at her. "I think I might leave it to Ferrut to go through your husband's scrolls today. He needs the experience. You and I shall have a nice chat."

Kashpot clicked his fingers. "Phixit, show Ferrut the way. I'll stay here with His

Eminence. Nofret, fetch us some wine!"

Nofret thrust the baby at Dad, who was leaning against a pillar with his eyes closed. Heebi Jeebi squirmed in Dad's arms and woke up VERY LOUDLY.

"She feels a bit squelchy . . ." said Dad.

Kashpot had a quick sniff. "I think Heebi Jeebi needs changing."

Ptoni thought of the hidden jewels. "No," he said quickly. "She's fine."

"She pongs."

"That's me," Ptoni blurted. "I fell into some mud."

Kashpot glared, but Grubbiflub chuckled. "Of course, it was you on that mudbank with the sinking boat! I thought the crocs would have snapped you up long ago."

He gave an extra loud burp as Nofret came back with a large jug, followed by servant girls

bearing trays of food. Rubbing his hands together, Grubbiflub settled down on the couch, and guzzled.

He guzzled heaps of little fried fishes (plus a jug of wine) . . . pigeon stew (plus two more jugs of wine) . . . roast antelope haunch (plus another jug of wine) . . . and lots and lots of honey cakes.

But finally Grubbiflub sat back with a loud belch, glistening with grease.

"Someone fan me."

Ptoni picked up the fan.

"Fan harder, you lazy oaf!"

"No need," said Dad, grinning wildly. He held out the cooling cone. "I got this from Widow Wignite's. It's made of the finest fats. You just put it on your head and, as it melts, fragrant oils trickle over the skin, giving the most cooling effect. Just like a mountain spring."

"You're pulling my leg," Grubbiflub sniffed.

"Oh no, they're the latest cool thing – worn by important people just like you, great sire."

"Rubbish."

"I've seen them," claimed Dad.

"And where would *you* have seen them?"

Dad looked slightly puzzled. Then his face cleared.

"I remember. At one of Kashpot's banquets."

"You've not been to one of my banquets. I couldn't afford to give banquets," said Kashpot quickly.

"Oh yes, you do," Dad blathered on, "at your country villa."

"You must have dreamt it," said Ptoni, fanning harder than ever.

Dad shook his head. "I can prove it!"

He suddenly pulled back the hangings, revealing the colourful murals. Sure enough, there was Kashpot, goggling at the dancing girls, with his guests all wearing their crazy cool cones.

For a long time nobody spoke.

The silence was only broken by the return of Ferrut, looking disappointed.

"His scrolls seem to balance," he grumbled.

"Who cares about boring old scrolls," said Grubbiflub happily, trying on the cool cone. "I always say that a picture's worth a thousand scrolls, and now we can see it for ourselves, thanks to our helpful friend."

"It's a pleasure," Dad grinned, "but don't thank me. They must have cost Kashpot a fortune."

Grubbiflub beamed, gave a nasty belch, and knocked back the last of his wine. "I agree! It's such a shame he was trying to hide them. He's been very naughty indeed, thinking he could cheat Pharaoh, so we'll just have to empty his store house."

"Bu . . . but . . ." Kashpot's jaw dropped open.

"Now I must rush," Grubbiflub said. "I'm late for my next appointment. Thanks for the snack, Mistress . . . er . . . Fretnot. I'll see you again next year."

As soon as the door was closed Kashpot turned on Phixit.

"I'm demoting you, bird-brain."

"It wasn't me who showed him –"

"You got those murals painted. Why didn't you ask that artist to paint me thin and hungry, and without any food on the table?"

"B – b – be reasonable, sire."

"You can be the new laundryman."

Phixit cringed. "No, Master. Please not the laundryman! Mercy!"

Kashpot turned on Dad. "As for you, you numb-skull, don't think you're trading with me now. I won't have any goods left! So you can stay stuck on that mudbank until the crocodiles climb on board and have you for their lunch."

"What did I do wrong?" protested Dad. "I thought I handled it rather well."

Ptoni followed Phixit out into the courtyard. He needed to clear his head, but the yard was as hot as an oven. Phixit glanced towards the river.

"I might as well jump in, and drown."

"It can't be *that* bad washing laundry."

"It is when it's done in the Nile. The last

two laundrymen both got chomped by crocs. I think I'll go to the temple and beg for mercy from Thoth. Do you want to come?"

Ptoni nodded.

When they reached the temple, everyone was milling about, bringing offerings for Thoth's feast. People were carrying bowls of beans, and plaster scarabs, and mummified ibises. There was even a mummified croc, which got Phixit into an even worse state.

A priest stood outside calling, "Roll up. Roll up. Gain virtue by giving to Thoth.

Fine wines especially welcome." But as they went through the entrance, another priest stepped into their path.

"No admission without an offering." He grabbed hold of Ptoni's box, and opened the

CHEAP GIFTS ROUND THE BACK

OFFERINGS FOR THOTH THIS WAY

lid. "Ah, figs," he said, peering inside.

"Careful! My scarab's in there."

"That will make for lucky figs. How thoughtful."

"Bring them over to me. I'd like a fig,"

called the High Priest. He was sitting with three other priests at a table heaped with food. Next to him was a fat man wearing a drippy cool cone on his head.

"Oh no," said Ptoni. "Grubbiflub!"

CHAPTER 7
THE UNLUCKY SCARAB

"Back out slowly," muttered Phixit.

But it was too late.

"You, boy," Grubbiflub called. "Come here. I need some more fanning."

Ptoni walked slowly over and picked up a fan.

"I've just been telling my friends here about your stupid father getting stuck on a mudbank, and helping me catch out Kashpot.

Pharaoh will be amused." He wiped a trickle of oil off the end of his nose. "I might even get promoted. But back to business, eh, Ferrut? This temple must pay its fair whack."

GRUBBIFLUB
OVERSEER
OF PHARAOH'S
DANCING GIRLS

"Care for a fig?" said the High Priest, hurriedly changing the subject.

Grubbiflub snatched two or three figs and popped them into his gob. He chewed. He scrunched, and then he shook his head so hard that he knocked off his cooling cone. He spat something out on the table. It was pulpy and green.

"What's *that*?"

"It *was* a scarab," said Ptoni.

"Booby-trapped figs!" shouted Grubbiflub. "One of you priests must have slipped it in."

"Whatever for?" asked the High Priest.

"To distract me from doing my lawful work. That's an offence. But I'll teach you."

The priests were wringing their hands. "Scarab beetles bring very good luck, sire."

"Not disgusting squashed ones like this," said Grubbiflub.

"How very true," said the High Priest in a deep solemn tone. "A squashed one is a Dire Warning of poverty, sickness and death."

"For whom?" Grubbiflub looked uneasy.

"For you, of course," thundered the High Priest. "You were the one who squashed it."

Oil trickled over Grubbiflub's eyelids. He blinked. "I never meant to!"

"A sign," the High Priest added, "that you must have done Bad Things."

"I've done nothing wrong. I'm a tax collector."

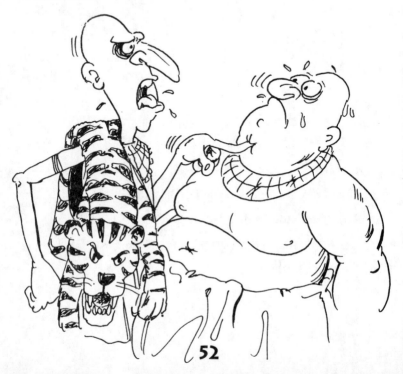

"Think carefully," said the High Priest. "Remember Thoth is the god of Scribes, so he will be listening to this."

Silence fell.

Ptoni looked around, then up at the statue of Thoth. The god of Scribes had a pot belly, long arms and a big ape-like head – very much like Kashpot. Not that looking so *godly* had carried much weight with the tax collector.

Though hold on . . .

Ptoni broke in, "I know what the tax collector did wrong!"

Everyone stared at him as if he was out of his head. He carried on in a calm voice. "The murals in Kashpot's house showed the god Thoth wearing jewels and enjoying some celebrations."

"Murals of our god Thoth?" cried the High Priest. "In Kashpot's palace?"

"That's right," said Phixit, catching on. "My Master is *so* religious, and Thoth is his Number One God and –"

"Hogwash!" yelled Grubbiflub. "Those pictures only showed Kashpot, that greedy grasping fat ape, stuffing his ugly face!"

The priests all drew in their breath.

"If that is what you think," said the High Priest, "no wonder Thoth is displeased."

"Thoth displeased? Oh no," stammered Grubbiflub, wiping the oil from his brow. "I never meant that. What should I do?"

"Action must be taken to avoid his wrath.

You've been too harsh to Kashpot. Take only a third of his stock, and give it to us."

"*You*?" said Grubbiflub.

"Of course – as an offering to Thoth."

"But I've got to have something for Pharaoh, or he'll sack me," Grubbiflub blubbered.

Ptoni had another idea. "I've got just the thing," he suggested. "A whole load of nice ripe melons."

"Oh no."

"Oh yes," said the High Priest. "And as a further penance, I think you should use your galley to get their boat off that mudbank."

CHAPTER 8
THE FEAST OF THOTH

And so it all came to pass.

Hefijuti was towed off the mudbank.

The stinking melons were loaded on to Grubbiflub's galley.

Dad got *twenty* bales of linen from Kashpot in return for his greasy palm oil.

Phixit got his job back.

And they all shared *the* most fabulous feast with music and dancing girls (and screaming Heebi Jeebi).

And everyone raised their goblets.

"To Thoth!"

"To Thoth!" they all roared.

"And to Ptoni," said Kashpot. "It was lucky he went to the temple."

"That's right. But the luckiest thing of all . . ." Dad slapped Kashpot hard on the back, "was that you looked just like a baboon."

Kashpot banged down his goblet.

"Calm down, Master," soothed Phixit. "Of course you're very lucky having such *godly* features, but," he winked at Ptoni, "I think the luckiest thing was your poor scarab beetle getting scrunched up by the tax collector."

"Didn't I say," Dad exclaimed, "that our scarab would bring us good luck?"

"Yes, Dad," Ptoni had to agree, "though not until it got scrunched."

"That's it!" Phixit raised his goblet. "It was the scrunch that fixed it. Let's all drink to the scrunched-up scarab!"

Trading

Money wasn't used in Ancient Egypt – everything had to be bartered. So if you were down to your last few beans you couldn't buy much for lunch.

Beer and Bread

Dad's lads had beer and bread for breakfast. Egyptians were very fond of beer and brewed their own from wheat or barley. The liquid  they produced was very thick and lumpy, so most people drank it straight from the jar with a drinking tube, leaving all the grotty bits at the bottom. The bread they ate often contained pieces of grit, so a lot of people had chipped or broken teeth.

Scribes and Tax Collectors

Egypt was an organised country and depended on written records. Since most people could not read or write, scribes were important people. If you were very clever, you could become a tax collector like Grubbiflub, responsible for collecting the state's taxes.

Baboons

Baboons are very intelligent monkeys, and the Egyptians trained them to do lots of tasks. Some animals were taught to climb up fig trees, pick the fruit and bring them back down. Others were used as sniffer dogs to police the local markets.

Thoth

Egyptians had many gods and goddesses. Thoth was the god of Scribes, and both the baboon and the ibis were sacred to him.

Feasts

Wealthy Egyptians like Kashpot loved giving enormous banquets with lots and lots of dishes. They didn't use knives and forks, so in between each course you had to wash your hands. If you drank too much a servant brought a bowl so that you could be sick.

Join Ptoni and his Dad up the Nile
in these other books.

THE MISSING MUMMY

07496 3650 5 (Hbk)   07496 3654 8 (Pbk)

Dad goes to collect some wine he is owed by Slosh, the
merchant. But poor Slosh has died, and someone has stolen his
mummy. It's up to Ptoni to find it, and to claim the wine.

THE FEARFUL PHARAOH

07496 3651 3 (Hbk)   07496 3655 6 (Pbk)

When Ptoni and Dad arrive at Pharaoh Armenlegup's palace,
they find the everyone busy preparing for a big Festival.
Unfortunately Dad breaks a law by mistake, and is sentenced to
be buried up to the neck in sand. Can Ptoni obtain a pardon
from the Fearful Pharaoh?

THE HELPFUL HIEROGLYPH

07496 3652 1 (Hbk)   07496 3656 4 (Pbk)

Dad decides that it's time Ptoni learnt to read and write, so he
hires an old scribe to teach him. Ptoni's new knowledge of
hieroglyphs helps him sort out a very peculiar mystery.